Genny in a Bottle

twelve ways to trick your biggest enemy

Kristen Kemp

an apple paperback

SCHOLASTIC INC.

New York   Toronto   London   Auckland   Sydney
Mexico City   New Delhi   Hong Kong

To Chandra Czape, who
is like my sister

No part of this work may be reproduced in whole or in part, or stored in a retrieval system, or transmitted in any form or by any means, electronic, mechanical, photocopying, recording, or otherwise, without written permission of the publisher. For information regarding permission, write to Scholastic Inc., Attention: Permissions Department, 555 Broadway, New York, NY 10012.

ISBN 0-439-21180-8

12 11 10 9 8 7 6 5 4 3 2 1   1 2 3 4 5 6/0

Printed in the U.S.A.   40
First Scholastic printing, February 2001

Chapter 1
"Welcome to My Life"
by Sophie

The word "win" is not in my vocabulary — for thousands of reasons.

I never won at musical chairs in the nursery school playroom. And forget scoring a piece of lemon meringue pie at the annual elementary school cakewalk — I never did it. Even at track-and-field day when I was in the sixth grade, I came in dead last in the hurdles — behind this chick who smoked me despite having a broken foot in a walking cast. Just last week — I'm a seventh grader now — I was rushing to get the last carton of cold milk in the lunchroom. Then guess what happened?! A sixth-grade boy pushed me out of the way, grabbed the milk, and ran away with it. The cafeteria lady handed me a warm, five-day-old carton and said, "Sorry, Sophie. But I found this in the back — you can have it. I don't want you to be thirsty."

Gee, thanks, I thought as I grabbed the warm,

1

sweaty carton. It tasted like melted, moldy cheese.

You think I'm exaggerating. I can assure you that I'm not. What I *am* doing, though, is feeling worse than a slug stuck in salt. And it's not just because of what happened at school today. Let me just tell you: As I was booking it to class before the bell rang, everyone scrambled in front of me. I lost my balance, fell down, and busted my kneecap on the stairway. I tried to act cool as an ice-cream cone — you know, like nothing had happened. But, of course, my hard-to-hide limp and bloody leg made my attempt to be discreet totally impossible. My white sneakers looked like evidence from a crime scene.

So, see, I never win. Now, that's not to say I'm a loser — not in the cool vs. popular sense, anyway. I am just this little wavy-haired girl who nobody really knows. It's not that I don't have friends — I have a few from band class where I play the piccolo — but I don't connect with anybody anymore. Most people like me and say hello; I just don't get into them all that much. I don't mind discovering great movies and songs all by myself, although sometimes I do wish I had a friend to discuss them with. Well, to be brutally honest, it would have been nice to have someone around to help me swab up my bloody knee. Or to talk to when I lose at kickball.

See, I used to have a best friend. We giggled and talked and had everything in common. She knew me so well that she could finish my thoughts for me before they popped into my brain. We were two peas in a pod for such a long time — in fact, no one alive on this earth today has known me for more years than she did, I mean does. See, *she* is my twin sister — her name is Jessica. We were inseparable until about a year ago.

That was when *things* started happening. Those *things* are the reasons I feel like a down-and-out slug now.

I know it wasn't my fault — I didn't change a bit. I am still, and always was, the same old girl who is clumsy, gets thrown out of sports-team tryouts (well, I really am not good at any of them), and just keeps to herself. That's my Sophie standard. But all of a sudden, Jessica became excellent at everything she did. For example, she tried out for track — and *presto!* she became the star of the 100-meter dash. She tried out for cheerleading, and next thing you know, she's the captain. She went out for basketball, swimming, and volleyball, and — you guessed it — she instantly became the best. She started to make new jock friends and stopped

3

hanging out with — or even talking to — me.

I was happy for her at first. I would go to her matches, games, meets, and whatevers to cheer her on. I sat with our parents and beamed as proudly as I could. Everyone was pleased as pears. But the more the 'rents gushed about her, the less enthusiastic I felt. Then things got really disgusting. Mom and Dad bought Jessica every piece of expensive equipment imaginable: rackets, balls, goggles, bloomers, and ten different kinds of tennis shoes. They didn't mind maxing out their credit cards. Jessica loved it — and became a snotty little wench. She thought more highly of herself than our parents did, if that was possible.

Through it all, I kept quiet. I sat back silently and watched it happen.

Everyone — Jess, Mom, and Dad — got more wrapped up in my sister by the nanosecond. They made her homemade PowerBars and ordered any takeout dinner she demanded. They went on and on about how special and talented she was. If they weren't talking to her, they were talking to other people *about* her. If they weren't at her sports events, they were out buying her a bunch of junk she didn't need.

Meanwhile, our parents didn't have much to say to me. Jessica didn't need me anymore, either. As far as my family goes, I became a cheap piece of Handi-Wrap. Things have been this way for a year.

And well, you know me. I already told you that I never, ever win anything. So when all of this started happening, I knew there was no way I could compete.

Chapter 2
"Boogie Down, Baby!"
by Genny the Genie

Hot hogmuffins!

Sorry to be so excited, but *j'aime* that song that just came on. Oh, sorry, that's French for *I love it!* I cranked up the stereo and boogied down in my bottle, where I have lived — and boogied — for the last thousand years. Sure, music may have changed over a millennium, but my undying love for it has not.

"You just keep on pushin' my love over the borderline," I sang out loud, even though my poor cat hates my rock-star-like voice. *"Doo-dee-doo."* I love that music — I could dance to it for decades. I know the chick who sings that song. I spent twenty-eight days with her when she was thirteen, as her genie. What a funky, spunky little diva. She couldn't stop trying on other people's clothes! She was such a fun handful.

Actually, my hands have been full a lot lately.

So many assignments — and I only have one ponytail. (You'll never see me wearing two! *So* not me.) I've been busier than a teacher at report card time. Busier than ever, really! But I love it. I travel all over the United States, my territory for the last few hundred years, and get all kinds of thirteen-year-olds out of their pickles. Maybe I've told you this before — but I tell so many stories that sometimes I forget who's heard what. Anyway, I am a genie, and my name is Genny.

I thought I'd better introduce myself before I start telling you about my latest calling. It's unlike any I have ever had before — and I've had thousands of callings. The thing about this one is, I don't know why it's so different. It's not different in a doomed, bad way. At least, I don't *think* it is. But there is definitely something about this one that's getting to me. I have a burning feeling deep in the pit of my big toe. It's tingling like a big bad headache, but it's in my toe, of course. That usually means something special is going to happen. I just wish I knew what. But I'm a genie, not a fortune-teller — and I am a terrible astrologer, although I really love the cosmos. Anyway, Catfish feels a strange vibe, too. He's been biting me a lot and begging for his Q-Tips with a new kind of urgency. Throttle (that's what I call my bottle) has been telling us we're loopy. I told him he was half-baked — and he got mad. (Well, he *was* baked over a fire 1,001 years ago!) He has been getting on my nerves because, really, what does he know? He never has feelings and premonitions about things like Catfish and I do. After all, he's just a bottle.

I should be nice to Throttle; he gets me to the places I need to go — though don't ask me how. His travel techniques are a mystery because I'm stuck in the bottle the whole time we're on the road. (There aren't even windows in here!) See, when I get a calling, he reads the signals with his radar. Then he speeds us to our do-good destinies. That's what he is doing right now. I wish I knew where I was going! I never know, though. I definitely don't have a choice when it comes to callings — I just get them and head out on my merry way. I don't tell my kid masters that, though. I like them to think they're superlucky (which they are!), and that I came to them because I wanted to. (I never, ever want them to think that *they're* the bosses.) But in reality, when a kid is really sad and really needs me, I have to go to them. It's my job.

I love my job! I still love it even when I have eerie, too-strange feelings about my assignments, like I do right now.

I was barely done dancing when we landed.

It was a smooth arrival, so Catfish and I gave Throttle kudos. (Last time we landed, he nearly knocked the breath out of us.) Then I heard someone playing some kind of instrument like a flute. I was definitely on Clouds Nine, Ten, and Eleven to hear — Pachelbel's music. The kid was playing an old piece called Canon in D Major. Ahhh, listening to the kid flute away was pure heaven. And oh, the memories. I remembered my best friend in France, my long-lost home country. I call it long-lost because it has changed so much. I mean, it's cool. But today's France is just as foreign to me as it is to you. In the last few hundred years, I have become quite the little American. But I easily morph into the culture of whatever country I am in.

I began humming along. I hoped for company to enjoy the music with, but Catfish just bit me and begged for Q-Tips. He even refused to dance — and you really need a partner when you hear beautiful music like that. I hoped my new kid master would rub me out of the bottle soon! I dreamed of dining on a fine slice of pepperoni pizza to go with the elegant, fancy music.

She played for three hours straight. I was surprised to realize how much time had gone by. I knew it had been at least that long, because I had hummed so much my vocal

9

cords ached. Then I began to burst inside. I kept thinking, *If you don't get me out of this bottle, I will eat my eyelashes!* Of course, I would rather be downing some pizza.

But the moment was so rudely interrupted. I didn't quite understand what I overheard, but it didn't sound good.

"Can you stop playing that pathetic, annoying junk you call music?" a teenage girl said.

Abruptly and sadly, the tunes faded and died.

"I thought you liked it," replied another girlie teenage voice.

"Well, I don't."

"You used to.

"I *used* to like you, too."

"Oh, please. Get out of my room, Jessica. You stink like sweat."

"Shut up. Anyway, Mom and Dad are sick of hearing that stuff, too. So stop."

"Are you deaf?"

"I wish I was. . . ."

"Just get OUT!"

Then the door slammed, and all was silent. Things were quiet except for the soft sounds of crying. Usually, that's my cue — sobs are the signs of teens in need.

I hoped Throttle put our bottle where the girl could see it. If not, I'd have to sit there all day helplessly listening to her cry. Nothing makes me go nuttier than that. I get all fruitcakey when I have things to do and I am trapped inside Throttle. All she had to do was rub three times and — *poof!* — Genny the Genie would be at her service.

Wait a minute!

She must've found us, because I was out. She wiped her eyes and looked at me. I was wearing a black fishnet top and a pair of black blue jeans in honor of Madonna and her first album. So maybe that's why this girl just kept staring at me.

Well, even if I wasn't properly dressed, I still had work to do. And by the looks of this sad and sobbing sweetheart, I knew I had to get started.

Chapter 3

"Oh, But Sophie *Is* a Winner!"

by Genny the Genie

If this little chick doesn't quit poking at me, I think I'll thwack her!

"You can't be real," she keeps saying between pokes.

"Ouch! I most certainly am," I said with impatience. I can't help it — the explanation part of this job wears me out every time. How many times am I going to have to tell these kids that they have their very own genie? I need to make a genie video training tape. Then I could just hit PLAY and be done with this part of the job all together. But since I had only just thought of doing that, I still had to go through all of the motions, slowly, with this new thirteen-year-old girl. I handed her the standard genie instruction book, let her read it, then explained the rules. I told her I don't do laundry, dishes, or homework. I offered to help with chemistry, but that's it. My cat and I also get pizza on demand. And Catfish needs Q-Tips, no questions asked. I told her all of the basic stuff.

She just looked at me, nodding. She didn't have any questions or comments. Well, she did say, "Wow! For me? Are you sure you're here for me?"

I replied, "Why wouldn't this all be for you?"

She said, "Because nothing is ever for me."

"Oh my," I said as I touched her hand.

She told me her name. It's Sophie. After I asked her who was making that beautiful music, she showed me her piccolo. I didn't admit it to her, but for a second, I thought maybe I'd been listening to a CD before. I just couldn't believe this girl had created such lovely sounds. I mean, she was so normal. She wore jeans and a T-shirt. Her brown hair was wavy. Her room was filled with stuffed animals and not much else. The walls were stark-naked white. She just looked, and I am so sorry to say it, kind of boring. Unlike the last few chicks I've spent time with, this one wasn't dynamic.

I hated myself for thinking these things. To make up for it, I quickly thought about all of the dynamos I had met in the past who had come in plain packages. Take Evelyn Ashford, for example — that chick could sprint. Or Emily Dickinson — she hid her true passionate self from everyone but me. They were far from boring. That made me think there must be something special about Sophie as well.

"Girl-*amie*, what did you do to your knee?" I asked.

She told me how she busted it going up the stairs of her school. She started crying again. She said she used to be best friends with her twin sister, Jessica — and now they hated each other. She told me that Jessica was the most back-stabbing and manipulative meanie she'd ever met.

"What does she do to you?"

"She ignores me."

Sophie didn't seem to want to explain further. I was dying to get the scoop, but it looked like I would have to wait for the juicy details. I am not good at waiting. Even more surprising, Sophie said that her parents can't stand her, but love Jessica. I found that really hard to believe. But of course, at first I didn't even believe the girl standing in front of me was playing Pachelbel's Canon in D Major.

"How do you know that?" I asked.

"They haven't talked to me in two weeks."

"No way."

"I'm serious. They haven't said anything besides 'Sophie, get out of the shower, I need to get in the bathroom.' Lately, I just wish they'd flush themselves.

"Everything around here is about who wins," she told me. "And I never win. Jessica does. Jessica is the best at everything. She's especially the best daughter. All I want is to win something. Anything. If I did that, my family would like me! The bottom line is that I just want them to love me again."

"Is that your wish?"

"I want that more than anything else in the whole world."

She didn't ask for millions or for boyfriends or even for popularity. That was unusual. At least I knew this was a sweet chick.

"Sophie, you're in luck. You're going to win this time because I can help you with those things."

I didn't have any clue how I was going to do it. But how could I not help this sweet, sobbing teen? I became determined to add sparkle to her life, help her bandage her knee better, and make her a winner — or at least get her in good with her family. I became completely inspired. Which didn't mean I knew *how* I was going to do it . . .

First on the agenda was some medication. "Sophie, do you have any aspirin?"

"Genies need aspirin?"

"Sometimes. Have any?"

"Yeah, but why?"

"I have this weird throbbing pain in my big toe. I can't get rid of it!"

If only I knew what in a crystal ball *that* meant.

Chapter 4
"I Have a Genie!"
by Sophie

Maybe it takes a few days to get used to having your own genie.

Mine limped around all night, complaining about her big toe. Then she went to bed early, saying she needed to get some sleep. Everything seemed fine to me — well, except that I had a supernatural being in my bedroom. At least some excitement was being thrown into my life. I told myself this was a good thing — not the usual kind of sucky stuff that goes on around me. Usually, the junk that happens to me jolts me like a whiff of warm, smelly milk. Like this weird guy at school named Andrew. He keeps smiling at me and talking to me. He is in my band class — and he is really freaking me out.

Genny is definitely a more positive force. Before she conked out, she told me all kinds of interesting stories. My favorite was learning about Queen Elizabeth I, the famous dame I've seen in some movies, when she was a thirteen-year-old like me. Genny also told me about her adventures in Hollywood on movie sets. Like one time, she became an extra so she could help destress her master Shirley Temple. See, Shirley had to work on two different flicks at one time! Poor thing. But Genny helped her sort everything out — fame, work, school, *and* a boy she really liked. Now that's cool! Genny even told me that Shirley used to sing "The Good Ship Lollipop" before they both went to sleep. Jess and I loved that movie when we were little — we watched it so many times in a row that our parents bought us matching head-phones so they wouldn't have to hear it any-more!

When I think about those times, I get sad. So I hope Genny can sort me out, too.

I was kinda tweaked when she said I was allowed to reveal her — my very own genie, and I still can't believe it — to two other people. She told me that usually kids tell their best friends their secrets. Every once in a while they tell their cousins or even their mothers. Well, I was upset when it dawned on me: I don't have anyone to talk to about Genny. She's so cool — like, way cooler than me — and I would love to let someone else know about her. But I don't have a best friend, close cousin, or a mom who would want to know my secrets. So I guess Genny will remain mine — and only mine.

Things weren't always that way for me. Jess and I had tons of friends. But as we got older, we stayed to ourselves more and more. We did that so much that eventually the other kids kind of stopped hanging out with us. We didn't care — it didn't even occur to us that we had lost our first- and second-grade friends. We just knew that we no longer played red rover on the playground, and we stayed away from hopscotch with the other girls. When everyone started sticker clubs, we didn't even want to be in one. We formed our own too-cool-for-school club. We didn't want *anyone* to be a part of *our* two-some. We were in our twins-only world. It's not that we didn't like other people — we really did. It was just that no one could understand us like we understood each other.

That was great and all — but that was when I thought sisters were forever. Now I know they're not. They're just as fussy as the friends you meet at the mall. One day you wear them like comfy Gap clothes and the next day you don't know them because they fit like those froufrou dresses at Express. My twin sister is that fickle. She dumped me like last year's fashion. I was out of style — all I'm good at is watching sitcoms and giggling at dumb jokes. Meanwhile, she was totally stylin' with her new blue ribbons in the 100-meter dash and every other sport imaginable. She didn't care about sports at all until a year ago. She always told me that they bored her. She must have lied. She lied about a lot of things, mostly about being best friends with me.

Well, what it all boils down to is one thing: I haven't had any friends except Jess since I was in kindergarten and had to share toys with other five-year-olds. I never thought I needed another friend. So I never made any. I don't ever win in social situations, either.

I hope Genny can help me. I am so confused. Do I need friends? I don't think so. Do I need my sister? No, I think I hate her. Do I want my parents to love me? Yes. But they won't unless I'm a winner like Jessica.

Chapter 5
"She Definitely Wins at Some Things"
by Genny the Genie

Oh, what a night! I tossed and turned — it was almost like I was trying to take a nap in a horse-drawn buggy. I woke up abruptly every five seconds — either Catfish was wrapped around my neck, making me bead up with sweat, or I was having a bad dream about other genies coming to get me. See, recently, there *was* a genie coming to get me — her name was Rebecca from Texas. I've slept better in cold, dark caves.

So it was a tough night in my new kid's bedroom, not that it was Sophie's fault. It was my own — I am more stressed than usual, and I don't know why. I just know it was impossible to sleep. Sophie was a sweetie — one of the nicest, most considerate kid masters I've had in a while. She fluffed up my pillows and aired out

21

my sheets. Then she gave me my own bed, since she's got a set of twins in her room. I was happy that I didn't have to cramp up inside Throttle on my crunched-up, 300-year-old mattress. I really need to replace that ratty old thing.

But before I give Throttle a much-needed interior makeover, I need to focus on Sophie. She has given me a pretty darn big assignment. Turning this weird little chick into a winner is no piece of birthday cake. The hardest part is going to be convincing Sophie that she is cool. How can she ever come out a winner when she doesn't think she's good enough for love, attention, and talent?

But she's smart, so I can definitely work with her. She knows a lot about everything, from my favorite soap opera to the shorthand names on the periodic table. I'm telling you, the girl is sharp. And she likes poetry — which is always a plus in my book. Sure, Sophie moped, and she obviously didn't feel very good about herself. But she also talked passionately about her favorite things, especially the new piccolo pieces she was trying to master. Then she told me something really intriguing: She wanted to write her own awesome tunes one day. I thought that showed some pretty major teenage ambition. She has been playing her instrument for only a year — she said she picked up the piccolo when her sister dissed her. But to hear her play, you'd think she'd been piping away for at least a decade! I'm not even pulling your strings — when she's playing, it is really so impressive.

Now, that is one thing that stumps me (and nothing much stumps me — I mean, I've heard just about everything before). I am really good at dancing to music — and, well, I admit it, I sing tunes badly — but I cannot write them to save my life. I have never tried to compose a sonata. If she had asked me to make a designer leather skirt, that would be different. But this girl isn't into those sorts of things. Writing music seems like something I need to learn, for her sake. So in the spirit of the best genies on this earth, I am going to consult the old Beethoven books on composing. I want to give her good music-writing direction; maybe that is something she'd be good at. But she doesn't *want* to be good at that stuff. She told me specifically that she wants to be good at sports.

The kind of sports my ancient French people played were a bit barbaric. I don't think you want to know what happened to the young boys when they lost. So I can't show her how to do the knight-in-shining-armor game or the spear-in-the-head triumph. Hmmm. I am not that good at sports; there's not much you can practice in a bottle.

Ahhh, but I do have a cat who, thankfully, reminds me of my talents. He must have heard me thinking — he brought me my old coo-coo ball.

That's a fun, unique kind of sport. I will teach Sophie confidence by helping her become a pro at the old coo-coo.

Now I just have to remember how to do it myself. . . .

Chapter 6
"She's Coo-coo if She Thinks I Can Do It"
by Sophie

I've been waking up every morning and playing the piccolo before I go to school. It's so exciting to have someone here who actually *asks* to hear it. I hope my sister and my parents are pulling their hairy moles off from listening to so much of it. I don't care — *I* am playing for Genny, the one person (well, genie) who really loves my music.

I wanted to play some more this afternoon before watching MTV, but Genny had another plan. She was bouncing around the room, kicking inanimate objects into the air.

"Sophie," she explained with her Genny the Genie kind of authority, "we are going to get you really good at something sportsy. This one is easy."

Part of me was really excited — all I want is

to excel at something. You know, so I can kick my sister's behind for once in my whole entire life. And maybe make my parents proud at the same time. But the other part of me was reluctant and terrified. I've heard that having your wisdom teeth yanked out by the roots is better than facing your worst fears. "Are you serious?" I asked. "I really rot at sports."

"Your wish was to be good. And this one's easy to crack." She bounced around the room and looked so bubbly. Her spirit was really moving me. You know, like a good piece of Bach — or maybe Prince (the artist formerly known as, or whoever the heck he is). I have been trying to play them both on my piccolo.

"Woohoo," Genny called, bouncing a little bean-filled soft leather ball around on her knees and ankles. "Look, this is called a coo-coo ball."

"Huh? What do you do with the thing?" My beat-up knee was just beginning to feel better. I didn't want to bust it up again with this nonsense. But it didn't look like I had much choice.

"Well, you bounce it around on your body and try to keep it off the floor."

"Genny, I've seen those before."

"Well, I know, I've seen 'em on television, too. They're cool!"

"Yes, they are. But they are called hackey sacks, not coo-coo balls. If you call it that, people might think you're, well, coo-coo."

"Sophie, you're the only one who can see or hear me, remember?"

"Oh, yeah."

"So as long as you don't think I'm crazy — I'm perfectly sane!"

"Genny, I think you're crazy."

She smiled and showed me the basics. We learned to bounce them on our toes first. I tripped twice, but I did get better. I did it and only tripped once. She told me I was doing great — that it would just take some practice.

Next, she showed me how to make the sack go from my toes to my knees. I don't know how I did it, but I thwacked myself on the head. Darn it, it hurt!

"Oh my goodness!" Genny yelled as she rubbed her neck with her fingers, then adjusted her ponytail. She seemed determined to teach me hackey sack even though I was quickly becoming hopelessly bad at it. For her sake, I tried and tried.

I batted that little hackey sack sucker from my white tennis shoe to my elbow. But I fell down in the process and knocked my stereo off its stand. It was a gallant try, and at least I didn't break my radio or CD player. I do have to give myself credit for that.

"Genny, I can't do this," I said.

"Nonsense!" We spent five more hours kicking that silly sack across the room.

"Genny, I'm really bad," I complained in the beginning when I hit Catfish with the bean-filled ball.

"You're not bad. You're awesome," she replied with way too much confidence. Has she ever seen me swim? I sink. Has she ever seen me on a balance beam? I always manage to fall off. Has she ever seen me play volleyball? I always wind up with a goose egg on my forehead. Now I do the hackey sack, and it looks like a demolition team came plowing through my room. Genny just didn't understand what she was getting into with me. But I wanted to be great — to find something I rocked at. So for another four hours, I just kept trying.

The final straw came around ten P.M. I still couldn't keep that ridiculous ball off the ground, not even with my toes. I would bounce it, and *plop*! It fell to the ground. Well, I got a little too excited with my toe bunt. I kicked it too high, it hit my mirror, and *BAM-SMASH*!

The mirror crashed to the ground in a million different pieces. In despair, we watched it fall.

"Sophie."

"Yes, Genny?"

"I didn't know a coo-coo ball — I mean a hackey sack — could break a mirror."

"I didn't, either."

Just then, Jessica came in to check out the commotion.

"What's going on here, loser? You've been making noise for hours."

"I have been busy, and I don't believe I have been bothering you."

"Oh, don't worry — you *always* bother me," Jessica said. Genny stood out of the way in the corner of the room. I could see her giving my sister the evil eye. Of course, my sister couldn't see her. But I wished she could. Maybe Jess would actually be jealous.

"Hackey sack? Is this how you broke your mirror?" She laughed out loud, Wicked Witch of the West–style, and I felt about one Barbie tall. Jess swiped Genny's coo-coo ball and ran down the hall. Our parents were sitting in the living room watching a tape of Jessica's last cheerleading pyramid. She tumbled into the room and hackey-sacked until they clapped. She bounced that dumb ball from her toes to her knees to her head and back to her heels. It was such a sick and disgusting play for attention. My parents ate it up — they nearly cracked their heads open crossways from smiling at her.

"I'm going to barf," I said as I marched back to my room, feeling like a total tool. At least

Genny saw everything, so she knows what I'm up against.

"Don't barf, girlfriend. Don't barf," she replied as she rubbed my back and adjusted her ponytail.

I couldn't help but cry a little as I got ready for bed. "I am so hopeless," I said over and over again.

Chapter 7
"Cats Are So High-Maintenance"
by Genny the Genie

I am not sure that I've ever had such a headache. Plus, I'm freaking out because my big toe is pounding like a broken blood vessel. I hope this doesn't mean Rebecca from Texas is coming back to torture me again via e-mail. I hope not! I'm too busy to deal with her right now.

It doesn't help that Sophie broke a mirror right in front of me. My superstitious side knows that bad luck is coming my way. No good will come to Sophie or Catfish, either, because they were in the room when it happened. I haven't seen a broken mirror since the year 1016. That year I saw more fire-breathing demons than I had ever seen before or have seen since — thank my Throttle. I need my mas-

31

ter wizard Papa right now. I must consult my spell books for an anti-broken-mirror spell or maybe a good luck charm. Oh, my goodness! I am so worried.

Catfish, my crazy companion, isn't helping matters. See, I always hated cats. But after spending a few years in here on my own, I accepted it when some nice old wizard gave me a pet. I guess I was glad; he does give me good company. It's just that most of the time we get along like wolves and chickens.

He brushed up against my leg and cried for more Q-Tips. He's had more of them in the last five days than he had in the last year! Something is definitely wrong with him. So I decided to give him another extra-special treat. I always turn him into a normal cat — instead of just a ghostlike genie cat — at least once during our assignments. He loves to do that. He can let off his literally bottled-up steam by chasing field mice and making nice with the lady felines. So I gave him this treat early. I did some magic — and *poof*! He was as real as any kitty I've ever seen. He was so happy that he danced around with me and didn't complain when I sang pop songs. He pranced around merrily.

Then, when I opened the door to let him out, he flew out the door like a streak of lightning.

That silly, crazy cat.

Chapter 8
"Life Is Good"
by Jessica

If Sophie doesn't stop it with that instrument, I am sure I will scream. She's doing it on purpose — driving me crazy with her flute. Or, *excuse me*, her piccolo. I call it her geek-o-lo. I say that to her just to get her going. I can tell it makes her really furious even though she rarely says anything back to me. She's like that — she doesn't like to start trouble with anyone. Not even me, which makes teasing her that much more fun.

My sister is just strange, and she drives me bananas. I can't believe I used to be best buddies with her. She feels sorry for herself all the time, and she always wants to be alone. She won't give the kids in her band class a chance — even though they want to be friends with her. She could have been involved in my sports teams — not that she's a good athlete like me, of course. But she could have been the softball

33

bat girl or the swim team manager. But no, she didn't want any part of that. She just wants to download music on her computer and play the geek-o-lo. She is annoying and boring, and I am through with her. We used to have so much in common, but we don't anymore. When you're in junior high school, you can't bond over Shirley Temple movies. You can't eat, sleep, and think the same thoughts as another person for your whole life — not even if you're twins.

I'm sure the fact that our parents like me better hasn't helped us. I think Sophie is jealous. But I can't help it if I have Mom and Dad all excited about me. I worked hard to make them feel that way! Besides, even if I hadn't tried to win them, they would have liked me better because I'm cool and interesting. Plus, I am a sports star and they are proud of me.

What does Sophie do? Not much, I'm telling you.

Like tonight, for example. She will sit up in her room while I win my races at the swim meet. Being the best is so supereasy. I love it because it makes me feel special and important, and I didn't feel that way before. In the past year, I found out that there is nothing I like more than winning.

But I am starting to like this fat and friendly

striped cat I found outside an awful lot. This furball is really cool. He came up to me when I walked into the house from school today. He meowed and meowed. So I took him up to my room where he — thankfully — stayed quiet. My parents may not let me keep him, so I put a cardboard box in my room and filled it with shredded newspaper instead of litter. Then I put a bowl of water and some leftover pizza in two dishes. That cat ate like he'd never been fed before — which he must have been, because he's huge. But anyway, he was really happy. He cuddled with me, and I fell in love. He seemed happy in my room with me, so that's where I will keep him.

Chapter 9
"My Little Secret"
by Genny the Genie

"Hi, I would like to speak to Mr. Schultz," I said into the phone before Sophie or anyone got home.

"Who is this, please?" the voice on the other end asked.

"This is Mrs. O'Bannon. I am Sophie O'Bannon's mom." Okay, so I lied! For a good reason, though, as you will soon see.

"Sophie who?"

"She is a student in Mr. Schultz's band class. I need to speak with him about her."

"Oh, okay. I just saw him walk by the office. Let me get him for you."

Mr. Schultz was a pretty cool man. I said to him, "I'm sure you know my daughter is getting very good at the piccolo."

"Oh, she is really coming along. The best music student I have seen in some five or six years."

"I am glad you agree. On that note, I have a request."

"Yes, Mrs. O'Bannon?"

"I think Sophie needs more challenge. Could you put her in the advanced band class?"

"We don't have an advanced class — but I was already thinking of promoting her into the eighth-grade band because she's so good. I will give her the news soon, Mrs. O'Bannon."

"I am so glad. As you know, my Sophie doesn't always realize how good she is."

"No, she doesn't. I think this will be a great experience for her."

"I do, too! Thank you, Mr. Schultz."

"Sure, you're very welcome."

"One more thing, though." I paused. "Could you please make sure that Sophie never finds out about this conversation?"

"Oh, I would never tell her! It will be our little secret."

Chapter 10
"I Have My Hands Full – Again!"
by Genny the Genie

Now I'm starting to understand. This Sophie chick is way too sweet for her own good. She does anything I ask her to, no questions asked. She listens to my stories, brings me slices of pepperoni pizza, and laughs at my jokes. I gave her a little test today — I told a really stupid joke.

"Okay, Sophie, knock, knock."

"Who's there?"

"Interrupting cow," I said.

"Interrupting cow wh — "

"Mooo!" I yelled.

She looked puzzled, then forced herself to laugh.

"Sophie, that was a dumb joke."

"Oh, no . . . it wasn't . . . really."

"It's okay, you don't have to laugh at me if I'm not funny."

"Okay. That's what I'll do, then."

I just pulled on my ponytail. In my experience, the supersweet ones can be the hardest chicks to figure out. The sugary ones have all of the same feelings as more outgoing, forceful girls, they just never show them. They don't want anyone to ever feel bad or worry about them. Well, I worry about Sophie.

"Sophie, do you know how great you are with that piccolo?"

"Oh, no, I'm not that good. You should hear the other kids in my class. They are much better than me."

"I doubt it, Sophie. I've known a lot of kids, and they're not gifted like you."

"No way. Anyhow, who wants to be good at the piccolo? No one likes the piccolo but me."

I let it go. I figured she'd find out she was great soon enough. Hopefully, I can convince her to be great at music and never try out for another sport again. We'll see.

I changed the subject. "Sophie, do you have any friends?"

She didn't answer me, really. Instead she said she sits with the band kids at lunch and stuff. She smiled at me and assured me she was fine.

Then she told me all about her day, and she talked about the things that are important to her, like her music, TV shows, favorite books, and even about stuff on the news. Sophie's really smart! She keeps me updated on all of the things going on in the world. Some of the recent discoveries floor me! I am amazed that you can see live pictures of Mars on the Internet whenever you want to. I mean, when I was a kid, we used to think the stars in the night sky were the gods' and spirits' nighttime candles. But hey, we also used to think that draining your blood cured headaches, too!

Anyway, Sophie is the best girlfriend any kid could have. She's much more talkative than Catfish, who has been gallivanting around so much that I think he has forgotten to come home! He deserves to have some fun, I guess. At least Sophie keeps me company. Every night, when she's done chatting, she politely asks me all about my day and my life. I know I talk too much because she is such an amazing listener. She even listens to my problems — like how I miss my family and my old boyfriend, Frederick.

I am lucky to have such a sweetie for a master! Anyone would be lucky to know Soph. But there has been only one phone call for her during the whole week I've been here — it was from a boy named Andrew. He just wanted to say hello to her. She flipped out and hung up on him.

"Sophie, is he a nice boy?"

"Yes — he's pretty cool, I guess."

"Then why won't you be buds with him?"

"I am scared to — I've never had any friends besides Jess."

"You have me!"

"Yes, I guess I do."

That thought seemed to surprise her.

Chapter 11
"I Finally Have Good News!"
by Sophie

"**O**h my goodness! Oh my goodness!" I ran into the house screaming for joy. I was worried that my parents would think I was crazy, so once I got into my room, I tried to keep quiet. That was really hard to do because I was so excited. Sometimes it's hard to talk to your genie and keep it a secret.

"Genny, guess what?"

She was sleeping on a pile of potato chip crumbs that were scattered all over the bed. But when she saw me, she bolted up. "Tell me, tell me!!!" she begged.

So I gave her my story. I had been put in the eighth-grade band class because my teacher, Mr. Schultz, thought I was so good.

"He even gave me the first chair, Genny!"

"The first what?"

"The first chair in band class is for the best person in the class. He put me in the best band class, then gave me the number-one spot in it! And I am only in seventh grade!"

"That's such great news!"

"I can't believe it! I am so excited. So excited."

Then I handed her a letter from Mr. Schultz. "Read this," I said. "You won't believe it."

She went over the note out loud. " 'Dear Mr. and Mrs. O'Bannon, I am so pleased to inform you that your daughter Sophie has been placed in the eighth-grade band class because of her masterful piccolo-playing skills.' Sophie, I told you that you are amazing! I am so happy!"

"Read the rest! Read the rest!"

" 'She is a wonderful musical student, as I'm sure you know, and I hope you are as proud of her as I am. I have even decided to put her in the top spot in the eighth-grade band. She has the first chair. We have a band competition next week in San Diego. I thought it would be a huge shame if Sophie wasn't allowed to go and help us win it. She truly is a treasure. Yours truly, Mr. Schultz.' I can't wait for you to show your parents!"

"Can you believe it? Can you? I'm gonna go show them now."

I marched into the living room right before Jess got home from whatever practice. I didn't want her stealing my one crescendo. My mom read the note, looked very pleased, then passed it along to my dad. I couldn't believe what happened next.

"Sophie, we are so very proud of you. This is the best news you could have given us," my mom said. "I am so sorry I complained about your playing. I had no idea you had gotten to be such an artist."

My dad even hugged me and said he couldn't wait to go to my next competition!

You don't know how happy I was when Jess walked in the room in the middle of all of this. Our parents gushed as they told her about it.

"Aren't you happy for your sister, Jessica?" my dad asked.

"Oh yeah, of course," she said as she stomped into her room. What a brat!

I didn't let it get to me too much. I just went into my room with Genny and celebrated.

I was so happy!

Chapter 12
"If Only Jess Were Sweeter"
by Genny the Genie

That Jessica is a baby. A bigger baby than my fat, spoiled cat. I haven't seen him much lately. He usually lets me know where he is. I am starting to worry. But I know he's just independent and strange. Sophie's parents are strange, too. As soon as she gets good at something and involved in a competition, they're happy with her! That's some major weirdness. But it seems to be what Sophie wants, so that's what I have to work for.

So she and I are getting down to business in the next few days. She's going to win the piccolo part of the band competition. I know because I have been studying all of my Beethoven technique books. I wanted to give her tons o' tune tips, but it seems as if she's already learned all of this stuff on her own. So

45

my job is to listen to her practice. The band will be traveling twenty minutes away to San Diego in three days. And this girl is gonna blow the whole city away.

Her parents have been asking her to play for them. This guy Andrew just keeps calling her on the phone — and she's actually taking his calls. And she hasn't busted her tail once on a step or a slab of concrete for a whole week! Things are going well, if I do say so myself.

That sister of hers, though, is just up to no good. She sulks around the house, shows up late for dinner, and comes in to gripe at Sophie whenever she can. Just last night, when Sophie was deep into practice, Jessica came in and said, "I have swim practice at six A.M. tomorrow morning, so I want you to shut up."

"You know the competition is coming up! I have to do this."

"You take your geek-o-lo and — "

What Jessica said was appalling. If I were Sophie, I would have been in her face telling her where to go. But not Sophie. She just got sad and started to cry. She asked me why her sister was so mean to her.

I didn't know the answer.

Chapter 13
"My Sister Stole My Parents"
by Jessica

I hate her!

She's doing all of this on purpose, I know she is.

She wants to steal away our parents' attention because she knows how much it will hurt. And it does hurt. Mom and Dad are even missing one of my meets so they can see Sophie play in San Diego tomorrow. I am dying inside, this hurts so much. I feel like I've been discarded! After everything I've accomplished at school . . . And Sophie just does one little thing. Then the whole world revolves around her.

I hate her!

At least I have this awesome cat to keep me company, since my parents don't care about me anymore. This furball, who I named Furball, doesn't leave my side from the second I come home until I leave the next day. I let him out during the day, while I'm at school, and I keep him with me every night. I don't know why I love this dumb thing so much, but I do.

I am glad he is here to keep me company lately. I've been crying into my pillow every night because Sophie is so mean. I am miserable. I feel like such a loser. I have so much pressure, I can't stand it! I have to get straight A's, win everything, and compete with my sister for my parents' attention! I can't handle all of this — and I am going crazy.

I petted Furball and cried some more.

Then I found this really neat thingy in my room. . . .

Chapter 14
"Who? You Mean Me?"
by Sophie

I got on the school bus to Qualcom Stadium in San Diego. All of the area high schools were going to be there, playing their instruments and hoping to win prizes. Our eighth-grade band — I am the only seventh grader in it — has been perfecting our pieces. We are pretty awesome at them. When we do "Ode to Joy" and "Boogie Beat" you wouldn't even think we're a junior high ensemble. Well, when you hear the trumpet section play alone you might. They sound like a bunch of car horns honking. I just hope I don't sound like that. I don't want to be the weak spot — something I am usually very comfortable being. Tonight, I have my very own important solo. I sure hope I don't blow it.

Before I left, Genny primped and pumped me up. I am not used to having my wavy brown hair fixed. It's blown out and styled just like I had been to the salon. I have on a teeny bit of makeup and a really cool blue dress that Genny made for me. She got me in a good mood by singing Madonna songs and dancing around. She asked me to play the piccolo for her — and I did it perfectly. I think I could play that thing while I'm in a deep, comalike sleep.

That doesn't mean that I am cool, calm, and collected about this competition. Asking me if I'm nervous would be as silly as asking if Beethoven was into music. I am so antsy that I've bitten off nine of my fingernails. Now it feels like pushing on little bruises every time I plunk the piccolo keys. Wow, there is more to being good at something than I thought.

So I get to the convention center at six in the evening and sit in a room with my band class while we wait for our turn. My parents are in the audience. I asked them to tape-record the whole thing. (For Genny, but I didn't tell them that.) They told me, nonsense — they would *video*tape it. I smiled so big, and then they hugged me. They advised me not to break a finger. Knowing me, that wasn't funny. Regardless, having them there was so cool and comfy. Jess, of course, didn't come — even though I went to all of her meets, matches, and whatevers when she first started in sports. But oh, well

— I guess she had some swim meet that she wouldn't miss for the world, or for her twin sister, either.

I sat and talked to the band class until it was time to go on. I was in my own universe when I played. It felt like the notes were coming from a secret place inside of me and landing magically onto the keys of my piccolo. I didn't miss a beat. And when I did my one-minute solo, I felt like I owned the world. I really don't know how the rest of our band did, I am just sure that I nailed my parts. It was the first time in my life that I ever felt so sure of something.

Of course, as I exited the stage, I flopped over and turned my heel because of the pretty platform shoes I was wearing. Sure, they looked good with my dress, but my feet throbbed worse than a pounding sinus headache. I think I sprained my ankle a little bit, but having my head in the clouds definitely dulled the discomfort. But now that I look back, I hope people were clapping because I played so well, not because my clumsiness made them laugh.

I went backstage with the band and waited for the other bands to play. Then I limped back in front of the audience with everyone while the powers that be announced the winners.

My heart sunk — we only got third place. I crossed my fingers hoping I would still win something for my solo. When the announcer called out, "In third place for the best soloist during a piece," I clenched my teeth. I wanted to win *something* so bad, more than ever in my life. I didn't get third. I didn't get second. Then I knew I'd lost.

The announcer came on again. "The first prize for best solo during a piece goes to Sophie O'Bannon and La Jolla Junior High School." This boy who bugs me all of the time named Andrew bumped me in the back.

"Sophie, that's you."

I just stood there, because I was sure I'd heard it wrong.

Everyone was clapping. I could hear my parents cheering the loudest. Mr. Schultz was hugging me. Suddenly I couldn't see — and my eyes just went dark. I passed out right there on the stage.

When I woke up my parents were hugging me in a room in the back. I was okay, so they started smiling and hugging me again. Mr. Schultz gave me a pat on the back and the trophy that I was supposed to have received on-stage. The guy named Andrew came in and told me, "Well, you did a great job. You didn't break a leg, but you nearly broke your ankle." It was sweet and funny this time when he teased me. We all giggled.

I went home in the back of my parents' car. I wanted to fall into a dead sleep, but I was too excited. They kept telling me how great I was. I went home, and Genny said the same thing. My evil sister didn't even congratulate me. Even that couldn't get to me that night.

I won something else as well. Genny told me her job was done.

"What?" I asked.

"Well, you know how I can only stay for twenty-eight days?"

"Yes?"

"There's one other rule."

"What?"

"I have to leave when my job is done."

"You do?"

"Yes, and now you're a winner, and your parents are completely into you. So that means there's nothing else for me to do here. The genie rule book says I have to go."

"You can't just hang around and be my friend for a little while?" I asked, very surprised at this oooh-yuck news.

"Well, I can stay for most of the day tomorrow, but then I have to leave, or I'll be in bigtime trouble. Plus, I've got to go to the genie doctor and have this big toe of mine looked at. It's still killing me!"

"You can't just leave me! Who will I share my

good news and fun with? Who will listen to me play the piccolo?"

"Sophie, you are now in the eighth-grade band — and you're their star player. You will have so many new friends that you won't have time for me anyway."

"You know that's not true," I said as Genny sighed and tightened her ponytail. If she left, none of this meant anything anymore. She was my new best friend. "Genny . . . I need you to stay. If I am your master, can I wish for you to stay?"

"Sophie, sweetie, let's just break the rules. I'm staying for a few more days."

"Really? Do you mean it?" The fact that she would do something like that for me was amazing. It made me feel really special.

"I mean it. I don't want to leave you, either."

She danced around while I played the piccolo. We celebrated! That was the best day and night of my whole entire life.

"Sophie?" Genny asked me as I finally wound down enough to go to bed. "Have you seen Catfish?"

I was sorry to tell her that I hadn't. He had been gone for way too long.

"That darn cat is really starting to worry me," Genny said.

I was worried, too.

Chapter 15
"That'll Take Care of Sophie"
by Jessica

I think I was born to be the best. Great things just happen to me over and over again. Like right before Sophie becomes a geek-a-lo star, I get my very own genie. I don't expect anyone to believe me, but I really did! My very own. I was crying and upset when I found this neat bottle that looked like it was from Target sitting on my desk. I picked it up and poked around. I rubbed it three times — and *poof*!

"Hey, babycakes! What's shakin'?" this girl with a southern drawl said.

That's how she greeted me as I proceeded to freak out. After a few hours, I learned that she is my genie, and I am her master. She told me to think of her like the woman on the Nick at Nite show *I Dream of Jeannie*. She said it was a lot like that.

And I knew exactly what I wanted to wish for. . . . There's nothing that makes me happier than being the best. (Well, Furball does, but that's different.)

She cackled when I told her that. I knew we were on the exact same wavelength. Things were definitely looking up, thanks to my good luck. And double thanks to my genie, Rebecca from Texas.

Chapter 16
"Welcome to Doom"
by Genny the Genie

Oh my . . . I think I must've had a seventh sense that I needed to stay on assignment with Sophie for a few more days. As it turns out, my work is just beginning. Things will definitely take the full twenty-eight days, if we can even fix them by then. Jumpin' Mexican beans — I'm telling you, this is terribly bad.

It's hard to believe things were so amazingly great just Friday, after the competition. My sweet kid master was winning, happy, and making friends again with her competition-crazy parents. Sure, she had a hurt ankle, but she didn't mind. She was still living on her favorite planet.

Then it happened.

The greatest thirteen-year-old piccolo player in the world (well, *I've* never seen one better — wait a minute, I've never met a piccolo player before!) . . . she got kicked out of band class!

Can you believe it? I can't. The last time I was this stumped was after I heard that Abraham Lincoln got shot. That was so shocking. And this is so sad that I would cut my blondish hair off if it would make things better.

Sophie came home bawling.

I hugged her and begged her to calm down enough to tell me what in a rat's nest happened.

"Iwas," snort, snort, "Iwastoldtogetout."

"What?"

"Mr. Schultz is so mad at me that he kicked me out. I might even get suspended."

"Oh my goodness! What on earth for?" Sophie is scared to kill mosquitoes even while they're biting her. I can't imagine that she would do something bad at school.

"Well, someone found Mr. Schultz's fancy clarinet in my locker."

"Your locker? You hate the clarinet!"

"I know! I can't stand those squeaky things. And now I'm accused of stealing one." She bawled really hard and wobbled around the room. I had to make her sit down so she wouldn't fall on her sprained ankle. "Mr. Schultz has this prize clarinet that belonged to some old dead guy. He always brags and tells us how great it is. So when he got to school today and it was missing, the school did a locker search. It was in my locker! What could I say?"

I had to sit down. Genies can't really cry — we're not supposed to get all emotional — but I have to admit, this one had me misting up. There's no way sweet, meek Sophie could do something like this. "I know you didn't, but I have to ask. Did you steal the thing?"

"No!"

I tried to hold her. It had already been a tough day — I am really missing my missing cat. Then this!

Mr. Schultz called Sophie's parents that night. He was livid, hurt, and in serious distress. He demanded an explanation. Then Sophie's parents lit into her — they were really unhappy. Meanwhile, my kid master basically has no energy left. She never told any of them that she didn't do it — I was screaming inside, I wanted to speak up for her so badly. I couldn't, of course, because no one can see or hear me but her. It was so awful.

That night, she said to me, "You know, Genny, all of this was too good to be true anyway."

"No, you remember that you won that prize because you're so good."

"They took that away from me, too."

"They are stupid," I said. Everyone was stupid. If anyone just got to know Sophie, they could see she isn't capable of thieving.

"I'm serious. I'm a loser, and I always will be. I am no good at anything I do. And everyone hates me."

"Pig feathers! Oh my goodness, Sophie. Don't you ever say that ever, ever, *ever* again. And don't you ever think I hate you." I had to take another aspirin for my big toe — and my pounding ponytail ache. As I peeked out Sophie's bedroom door, I couldn't help but notice that Jessica was hanging around the hallway looking mighty happy.

Something was up with that sinister sister.

Chapter 17
"I Hate Me"
by Sophie

I hate my life. My whole existence is just one big fat 200-pound kick in the tail. I think I could cry for two days straight. Wait a minute — I know that's exactly what I'm going to do. The one time I have been able to feel happy in the whole last year gets ruined, then totally stripped away. I can't even stay on top when I'm finally there. I fall miserably to the rock bottom. I'm worse at winning that I am at losing.

It hurts all the worse because my parents aren't speaking to me. After hurling yells at me for four hours straight — my mom was crying like I was — they told me they couldn't stand to look at me anymore. They demanded that I stay in my room — like I was even considering coming out. Then my mom brought me a bowl of stale granola with nasty warm milk for dinner. Genny was appalled. She said even a sad girl had to eat. She had some pizza hidden inside

Throttle in her genie fridge. She begged me to eat it. I nibbled, even though eating was as appealing as throwing myself into the mouth of a hungry great white shark.

Genny is superupset, I can tell. At least I have one person (well, genie) on my side. I don't know what I would do without her here. And it made me feel a little better when my kinda-sorta friend Andrew called me tonight. He said he hoped everything got cleared up soon because he'd miss me in band class. He told me he knew I didn't do it. It felt nice to hear it — even though it was weird to hear it from him. The guy is a total music nerd — but he's cute. He wears nice clothes, smells like expensive cologne, and has curly hair. More than that, though, as much as I tried to avoid him, he's completely cool. We can talk for hours about nothing. Well, that is, if I let him talk to me. New people in my life freak me out. Anyway, tonight I let him talk. I liked what he was saying.

I am not sure I liked what Genny said later. The thought she brought up nearly made me sick to my empty stomach. "Sophie, do you think Jessica did this to you?"

"Jess? She's got nothing to do with this. Although I bet she's thrilled that I'm in the dog-house, and she gets to be the good sister."

"She looked gleeful when you got home from school," Genny went on. "I don't mean to upset you more, *mon amie*."

"I don't think she'd be *happy* because I'm in trouble. What are you trying to say?"

"I wonder if your twin sister, well, stole that clarinet and put it in your locker. Does she have your combination?"

"Yes, but she would never do that to me! I'm sure of it!" I couldn't bear to even think about it. Jess wouldn't. She just *wouldn't*.

Chapter 18

"Nightmares Are Better Than This"

by Genny the Genie

Some snooping around was definitely in order, if anyone was ever going to get to the bottom of this mean and hateful matter. Sophie wasn't going to do it, that was for sure. She was content to sit back and take the rap for a crime she didn't commit. Well, she's my kid master, and she is my friend. If she won't do anything about it, I will. I have a job to do, and I have never left an assignment undone. Ever! I have only just less than two weeks left with Sophie, and I'll be an out-of-work genie before I leave that girl in a pickle.

Sophie refuses to suspect her sister of anything. Or if she did, she would never admit it. I, on the other hand, have a fishy feeling about her fraternal twin. That competitive spotlight-stealer better get ready to meet her match! If I can take on earth-destroying demons — which I did in the year 1065 — I can take on that star swimmer at La Jolla Junior High.

Of course, first I have to make sure she did what I think she did. I wouldn't want to get her into trouble unless she deserved it. So I set out to do some private investigating. But what I saw was worse than anything I've seen in my whole entire, way-too-long life. This is when I needed my cat — he could've found this out so I wouldn't have seen it in person (well, in genie, to be correct). But he was nowhere to be found — another major malfunction in this assignment. I don't want to admit that I miss the furball. But I do — and I have a feeling he's in trouble. I need him!!! I am in a pickle, too!

Here's what happened: Jessica was having a ball, jumping on a pogo stick in her bedroom. She was always doing something hyper and jittery in there, so I didn't think much about it. I did find it strange, however, that she was talking to herself. She was very involved in a conversation, but I didn't hear anyone's voice except hers. Deep in my heart, I knew what that meant. I just didn't think it would be a big deal.

It was — I mean, it is. I wish I knew what to do!

I watched her talk while I strained to hear what she said. I didn't want to march into her room. See, I usually won't enter someone's private space while I'm staying in my kid master's house. That's what ghosts do, not genies. I am not on this earth to haunt or torment people. So when I'm on assignment, I generally stay out of other people's business. I mean, I *could* watch them all the time because it's not like anyone can see or hear me, but that's not my job. Nor is it right. But this time I made an exception to the rule. I suspected Jess of doing something really mean. To get to the bottom of it, I needed to get into her mind and her room.

She was saying, "Well, maybe we could do that. I don't know."

I heard a muffled voice — kind of like a radio station coming in and out — saying, "Let me make all the decisions. If I were you, I wouldn't question what I say."

"Well, I guess you're right," Jess said. Where's that girl's backbone? And who was talking to her that way?

After listening really closely, I could barely pick up the other voice — a chick's voice with a southern accent. My ears pricked up and began to tingle. My toe throbbed, shooting pain all the way up to my earlobes. I walked behind Jessica. Her back was to me as she jumped around on the pogo stick. Standing straight across, face-to-face from me, was . . . *Oh my goodness! Oh my goodness! I am so scared!*

It had to be another genie! I haven't laid eyes on one in decades. But sure as the sky is gray when it rains, another girl just like me was staring me down. That shouldn't be a problem, but I knew this one was bad because my toe and stomach killed. Plus, it was obvious that she wasn't going to do the genie greeting ritual. It's a by-the-book hello we genies do to each other. Sure, it was impossible to do our hellos because Jessica could see *her*, and not me. But I could tell by the way this genie looked at me with those dark, mean eyes that this wasn't going to be a friendly genie meeting.

"Hey, what are you looking at?"

"Nothing, Jess. Nothing at all." She glared at me. She definitely had a cowgirl accent. "Listen, could you fetch me a diet Coke? I am *so* parched."

"Um, okay." Jessica left the room, and I inched toward the door. I didn't want to be attacked — especially without Catfish or Throttle there to help me.

I put my hand out and began to do the ritual "hello, hello" dance. I didn't want to do it, but it was an ancient rule I wasn't about to break.

"Oh, please. That is *so* last century. Besides, if

you know what's good for you, you'll stay out of my path. . . . Well, really it doesn't matter what you do, Genny. You and your old-fashioned ways won't be around much longer."

"How did you know who I am?" I mean, most genies have heard of me — after all, I am the Year 1000 genie and very famous. But they don't know what I look like!

"Don't you know me, sweet tea?"

"Call me sweet tea again, and that's the end of your cowgirl hat."

"You don't scare me."

Then it dawned on me. I knew who she was. I was terrified, but I know a good genie never shows it. I could never beat down evil kings and head-chopping queens by acting like a pussycat. So I looked her dead in the eye and said, "Don't even think about it, you slimy rat-trap. Stay out of my way — I mean it, Rebecca from Texas."

I snapped my fingers, wiggled my hips, and *poof*! I disappeared into the safety of Throttle. I shook uncontrollably all over — even my eyelids were quivering. I could feel how strong-willed and powerful that genie-girl was. There was always something unique about a millennial genie — and she was the new supposedly special one, the Year 2000 genie. There was *something* about her, all right. I felt pure evil oozing out of her pupils.

I have seen evil before, just never, ever from another genie. Let me tell you, though, I will die before a brand-new lowlife genie beats me. Or gives the geniehood a bad reputation. I will *die* before that happens. That is the truth.

I just hope that cheesy-smelling, double-processed bleached-blond chicken couldn't see how scared I was.

Chapter 19

"How Much Can
I Juggle?"

by Sophie

I am not sure if anyone has ever stopped by my house to see me. I guess there's a first time for everything, because it happened today. My friend — did I just call him a friend? — Andrew knocked on my door after school today, before my parents or anyone else got home. I don't even know where Genny was. He rang the doorbell, so I looked out my bedroom window. I could see his sand-colored curly hair and his bike outside. He was carrying his saxophone in a case on his back.

I was very tempted to pretend I wasn't home.

"Sophie, I know you're in there — I just saw you walk in," Andrew yelled from outside.

Busted, I walked down the hall and opened the door. My heart acted like it might split in half and pop out of each ear.

70

"Hi."

"Ahhh, you're home," he said.

"Yes, I'm home."

"Here, I have something for you." He handed me a card in an envelope.

"What's this?"

"Open it."

I did, and there was Snoopy falling off a bike. The card read, "Don't let the bumps get you down." Andrew wrote underneath it, "Let me know if you need a friend. You are the coolest person I've ever met, Andrew."

"Thanks," I replied. My heart was still acting up from nerves, and now my armpits were each becoming wading pools.

"You're welcome. I mean it."

"I need this right now."

"Okay, well, I'll see you at school tomorrow. I was kinda hoping you'd practice our new music with me during lunch period. I don't want you to get behind in band class, even though you're not in it right now."

I perked up — that sounded exciting. "I, uh, I'd love to."

"I'll see you there tomorrow." And he was gone.

I ran up to my room, desperate to find Genny. I needed some advice! Does this boy like me? Are we just friends? I hope we're just friends, really. The thought of being boyfriend-girlfriend with someone flips me out. But I'm not so freaked at the thought of having a new pal. I think getting so close to my genie has helped me with that. Speaking of, where is she?

I walked into my room. Oh-my-goodness, I was glad to find Genny sitting on her twin bed. But it wasn't a good sign that she looked so sad. She hung her head down toward her lap. She had knots in her long blondish hair and was busy tying several more. The scene was pathetic!

"What's wrong?" I asked.

The way she looked at me was weird. I'd never seen her so scared — usually she's my self-confident genie who sparkles so much she could light up a room. She worried me. "Are you okay, Genny?"

She didn't say anything. She looked like she might cry. Then she said, "I can't find my cat."

I'd do anything for her, so I looked all over for that furball. He wasn't anywhere to be found.

Chapter 20
"Rebecca Is a Gift from the Gods"
by Jessica

Getting my own genie is right up there with becoming captain of the cheerleading squad — it's one of the best things that's ever happened in my whole entire life. Rebecca makes me feel like a princess. She always tells me how great I am and lavishes me with presents. She comes up with thousands of ideas on how I can win at all of my sports activities, and even better, how to get my mom and dad to like me best again. I may not like everything she does. But I have to hand it to her — it always works.

Besides, I like her. She's always there for me — unlike my new friends at school. I know lots of guys and girls from my sports teams, but I've only known them for a year. They have their own inside jokes and parties. Sometimes I just don't feel like I connect with them. Don't get me wrong, I have mucho fun when we all hang out, but I don't totally trust them or feel like I can be my real self with them. My sister used to know me better than I knew myself, but Sophie and I are over. Now, at least, I feel like I have a best friend again. I do think Rebecca understands me.

She knows exactly how I feel. I can't stand losing — and she can't, either. I want everything in sight, and since she knows what that's like, she gets me everything. Now my closets and other secret hiding spots are crammed with so much new stuff — scooters, skateboards, cheerleading outfits, swimsuits, goggles, and balls — that I don't know what to do with them all. I often just take them out and admire everything.

I feel like the luckiest girl on earth. Well, I've felt like that a lot. I just got down when Sophie stole my spotlight — but then Rebecca came and things are much, much better. Well, usually they're better. While we do have nonstop fun, Rebecca and I argue a lot, too.

We did today. I didn't like it when Rebecca said, "I know what I want to do to really mess up your sister Sophie."

"Rebecca, I don't want to mess up her life, I just want to be the best daughter in our family.

I just want to make sure she doesn't steal my thunder. More importantly, I must win at everything I ever do."

"Yeah, yeah," she said. "So anyway, I want you to go in Sophie's room and look for a cute little ancient artifact in there. It's a bottle — and it looks something like the one I arrived in, but much older and yuckier. Steal it, because I have been spying on her and I know she loves it. You want her to cry when it's gone."

"No, no. I don't want to do things like that to her."

"Well, do you want my help or not?"

"I do, Rebecca, but I'm the one who gets the final say, right? I don't mean to be rude," I explained as politically as I could — my genie has a temper that I didn't want to set off. "But I don't want to do things like that to Sophie."

"Well, if you don't listen to my advice, I'm not sure I can help you."

"I didn't even like it that you stole the band teacher's clarinet and framed Sophie for it."

"Well, you got what you wanted, right?"

"I guess."

"Then shut up," she said with a defiant southern accent. Afterward she made some awesome food for me. And she hooked up a new game system to my TV. "Jess, let's not fight anymore, okay?" she said later. "Let's just have some fun tonight."

"Okay." That sounded good to me. We played video games all night long. The only bummer was, Rebecca usually won.

Chapter 21
"Another Dog Day"
by Genny the Genie

I have enough problems and worries. I need my cat back. He has been with me for 997 years. I know his every purr. And as much as Catfish gets on my nerves, I don't like my life without him sleeping beside me at night. Enough is enough. I have to find that darn cat. I have to get to the bottom of whatever is going on!

Sophie came home from school and moped around. I think it's terrible the way her parents won't speak to her. Her favorite band teacher has thrown her out. And she is so upset about it that she won't even play the piccolo for me. She's been feeling miserable for a few days. I am sure I haven't been much help, either — I've got an evil genie living in the room right next to me! Speaking of Rebecca, I got a nasty little note today slipped underneath the door:

Dear Genny the Antique Genie,
Keep a close watch on your bottle. I do plan to
take it and break it.
The war is on, sweet tea. And I will win.
Yours truly,
Rebecca from Texas

Making a bottle threat is a very low blow. No genie can survive without her little glass home. She really peeved me by even bringing it up. But she also made me laugh. That's the oldest trick in the book — she'd know that if she'd been a genie for at least one full year. Still, because she is so new and clueless, her threats are all the more frightening. When someone doesn't know what's going on, they can be that much more evil.

I haven't told Sophie about this because I'm here to help her, not vice versa. She doesn't need the extra stress yet. My salt-on-a-wound mood is already doing a number on her. She just asked me yesterday why we haven't been dancing around the room. I don't have a happy bone in my body right now — instead, my insides are ice cubes. All I seem to care to do is eat potato chips and tie my hair in knots.

I am done freaking and worrying and taking what this mean genie dishes out. The old spunky world-saving Genny is back.

I would just feel better if I found my cat.

"Sophie," I said as she plopped down in front of MTV.

"What, Genny? Do you want me to get the knots out of your hair again?"

"Well, yes. Later, though. I need your help with something first."

"I can't help you with anything. I'm a loser."

"You are the best thirteen-year-old piccolo player in the world. You are so incredibly sweet — "

"I get it," she said.

" — that I know you'll take me to all of the neighborhood back alleys and woods. I have to find my cat!"

Since it's getting cold outside, the nights are getting shorter. That meant we had to move fast.

"Kitty, kitty, kitty," we yelled as we walked all through her neighborhood, in the Mission Boulevard section of La Jolla. We made lots of feline friends, but we never found Catfish. We went near the school, where there is a big field and a small patch of woods.

"I've seen lots of mice around our cafeteria, so maybe we'll find him here," she said.

Sophie thought she spotted him that night, so she started running toward a kinda-faraway tree. "Catfish, Catfish!" Then, *blam!* — she nose-dove into the parking lot, just before the concrete turned into nice, soft grass.

She started to weep. Her other knee was a crime scene.

"Genny, I lose at everything. I can't help you find your cat. I can't even do that for you. I can't win a contest and keep the prize. I can't be promoted to the eighth-grade band and even be allowed to stay in it. I am broken all over."

I rubbed her back and bandaged her knee with my headband. It was a cute headband, but patching up her bloody knee was more important than my vanity. I told her I loved her and walked over to the tree.

There was no Catfish to be found.

I was starting to wonder if I could win against Rebecca without him. Maybe I had been on this earth too long. Maybe I had gotten rusty. Maybe I was the biggest loser of them all.

When we got back to Sophie's minus my Catfish, we both felt chewed up and spit out. I played my CDs to cheer her up. I don't think it worked; she just cried and went to sleep.

I checked my genie-mail that night, hoping a letter from a long-lost friend might just lift my sagging spirits.

All I got was an e-mail from Rebecca from Texas. It began with two heart-wrenching words:
Meow. Meow.

Then it said she had taken him as her own genie cat. "He will live in my bottle forever," she wrote to me. Stuff like this doesn't happen to genies, but that made me cry and cry. I couldn't stand the thought of something bad happening to Catfish. And if he was trapped in her bottle, I couldn't just yank him out. It's very dangerous to go into a genie's bottle — it's very hard to get out. This hurt me through and through. But after I boo-hooed, I changed my tune. I was steaming, hair-straightening furious. She had broken the genies' can't-be-mean rule for the last time. She was messing with my kid and my cat!

Live in her bottle forever? Only over my dead genie body.

Chapter 22
"Meet the Real Genny"
by Genny the Genie

No one messes with my cat. Any fear I felt is gone — it has been replaced with total, complete, planet-exploding rage.

I don't care what it costs me — that genie is going down. She is breaking the rules. Meanness is a genie's biggest sin in the universe. But I don't know if the rules apply anymore. I know I'll do whatever it takes to beat her at her own evil game. I flipped through my secret weapon, my very first *Tips for Genies* book. It is 10,000 pages long, so it took me a while to find what I needed. Oh, but I found it. There was a chapter called "Twelve Ways to Trick Your Biggest Enemy."

It was filled with the most interesting advice you've ever heard. Just listen to some of these old-fashioned tips (some have been updated, as you'll see below). You'll understand why I was earlobe-deep into my re-search.

1. Turn enemy into a frog.

Rub the wart of a stinking toad that weighs at least one pound onto foe. Foe will turn into a frog immediately. Keep your foe as your pet. The nicer you are to your frog foe, the better and longer your whole life will be.

2. Make enemy disappear.

First go to Egypt and visit the tomb of King Tut. There you will find a little old psychic named Esme selling things outside. Tell her the secret password, "Trix are for kids," and she will reveal herself as what she really is: a powerful, good witch. She will respond, "Ahhh, yes. What can I do for you?" That's when you tell her you need the Digestive Dust of Disappearance. She will hand you a teaspoonful. (Do not rub your mouth after handling it!) Give her a warm hug — that's how she expects to be paid — and go to the land where your enemy lives. Slip some of the dust into your enemy's cheese (or veggie) burger. She will vanish into thin air for the next one thousand years. You will not see her again until then.

3. Make enemy watch *Charlie's Angels* reruns.

Tie your foe down to a comfortable chair. Make her view at least six days' worth of this television show in a row. She will thus go insane and will no longer be your problem.

4. Feed enemy to the world's hungriest tree sloths.

Capture foe and go to the far reaches of the Antarctic. In the farthest northwest point you will find a sign that says THIS WAY FOR ENEMY-EATING TREE SLOTHS. With enemy close in toe, follow the signs. Leave enemy there and go back home. (Note: This remedy is only acceptable if your enemy has threatened your life. If you feel bad about feeding her to animals, remind yourself that the tree sloths in Antarctica are starving.)

5. Give enemy new home in faraway place.

If your antagonist lives in a cave, take ancient rock-blasting machine into enemy's home when enemy isn't there. Blast her dwelling. Then make sure you send her a notice that a beautiful castle is waiting for her on the opposite side of the world from you. Enemy will definitely get out of your ponytail, although you must provide the mansion on the opposite side of the world.

6. Make enemy be nice.

Collect twenty-five years of *Peanuts* comic strips. Handcuff your foe to a nice, soft, comfortable couch and read the funnies to her. Make her look at pictures of Charlie Brown, Snoopy, and their friends frequently. She will come out of this therapy a kinder, gentler person — and probably will turn into your friend instead of enemy.

7. Turn the world against enemy.

Go to your bathtub and fill it with blood-warm water and a wine spell draught. Then chant this spell, "The world is against [insert enemy's name]," four hundred times. Drain the water, then clean tub with Comet. Within three days, every person in the world will completely ignore your enemy. Then your enemy will come to you begging you not to ignore her. She will probably offer to do anything as long as you'll be her friend.

8. Employ the universal rules of good karma.

Say your enemy is female. Hunt for your foe's best male match (probably someone who is as sinister as she is). Set them up on a date. Cast love spells from *Valentine's Ancient Spell Book* for ten nights straight. Your biggest enemies will be married within the year. If you have spent your own life being a good person, and they have each spent their lives making other people miserable, the following will happen: They will make each other miserable forever and ever. They will be too miserable to ever bother you again.

9. Take enemy to Texas.

This will only work if your enemy is a criminal. When she does illegal acts in that state, she will get caught promptly and the Texans will lock her up in prison for the rest of her life. The only way she can bother you is through the U.S. mail.

10. Make enemy pay you big money.

Feed your enemy some pepperoni pizza. Then cast the pepperoni addiction spell on her from the *Ancient Book of Witty Pranks*. Next make sure she can't ever get her hands on pepperoni pizza or anything made with pepperoni again. Show her that you are her only source for pepperoni in the whole world. (You may have to buy up all of the pepperoni in your state.) Then tell her she can buy some pepperoni from you, but only at a very high cost.

11. Trick enemy into thinking you like her.

Bring her four of your very favorite outfits, making sure you steal four of her hairs from her brush for later. Boil her hairs over a fire while you chant, "I turn my friends into enemies. I make them my long-lost bosom buddies." She will call you in the morning and ask you to lunch. Go to lunch amd make nice. Compliment her a lot and listen to her talk about whatever she wants. She'll think you and she are friends and will never do anything mean to you again.

12. Make enemy worry about her mother knowing so much.

Ask a fortune-teller to give your enemy a free reading. Have fortune-teller tell your enemy, "[Insert enemy's name], if you're not nice to [your name] for the rest of your life, your mother will know every single thing you do for the rest of your life (especially the mischievous stuff)." Of course, you may need to pay off the fortune-teller, but it will be worth it. Your enemy will cease torturing you.

The ancient books were so helpful! I got some great ideas.

As an old wizard once told me, "May the best genie win."

Chapter 23
"Another Kick in the Tail"
by Sophie

I have one thing planned on one day in my entire lifetime, and this happens. It's unbelievable. I finally told this boy Andrew that I would stay after school for a few hours and practice with him. He's getting really good at the saxophone, and I need to keep up on my piccolo playing, I finally realized. So we've been going over what he's doing in the eighth-grade band class. He's really fun, and I'm not getting that strange love vibe from him anymore. Or at least he's laying off it for a while. I'm glad, because we are becoming really good friends. We can talk for hours, and there are no weird silences. We love to discuss music and school and our families. He has issues with his parents, too. But at least his parents will speak to him.

All my mom has said in a week is, "Sophie, practice your piccolo." I'm not grounded or anything — they probably didn't ground me because I never leave home as it is. But they just gush about Jessica in front of me. Then they tell me they're still mad at me. I didn't even steal Mr. Schultz's clarinet! I finally got up the nerve to tell my mom — and you know what she said? "Sophie, I can't ever forgive you for this unless you admit your mistakes and apologize for them." So here I am, all ready to write a big, gushy I'm-sorry letter to my teacher and my parents. But Genny won't let me. She says just to sit back and wait a few days. I can tell she has something up her sleeve. I can tell a lot is going on with her. But I don't want to press her — I know she'll tell me when she's ready.

I just hope whatever she's planning is a doozy. And I hope it goes down soon.

That sister of mine is much meaner than I ever dreamed. I think I am ready for paybacks — I don't have to play fair anymore. Not after tonight.

So like I said in the beginning, I was plunking away with my new friend Andrew, and I didn't get home from school until six. I took one step inside the front door. My mom was standing there. "Where have you been?"

I explained everything, thinking she'd be

happy that I was trying to keep up with the piccolo.

"Well, young lady, that is the worst excuse I've ever heard. We had plans to have a nice family dinner. Your sister made up these sweet invitations on the computer and said she'd make the whole thing. I saw yours lying on the kitchen table last week. Then what do you do? You don't bother to show up!"

"Mom, I didn't get it."

"I'm supposed to believe you? Get your tail in the kitchen and clean it up."

I marched into the kitchen — it was a total disaster. Whatever she had made — it looked like a terrible attempt at fried chicken — was all over the place. The countertops and floor were covered with flour and eggs. The pans were filled with grease, and the sink was filled with mixing bowls, chicken bones, and plates. Clean this up? They might as well have asked me to raise the dead. And do you think there was any food left for starving me? Not a crumb. Not a bite.

That little wench. She knows I was never invited to this dinner. Why would she want to hurt me this way? They already like her better. She already wins everything in the world. I never knew this terrible side of my sister. I am so sad I will cry. But I am tired of crying.

I had a long time to think while I cleaned up that kitchen. It took me all night. When I was done, I decided that I'm tired of sitting back and taking it — especially if Jess planted that clarinet in my locker. I told Genny I wanted to do something about this.

She got so fired up she started to scare me.

Chapter 24
"I've Got It!"
by Genny the Genie

This isn't just about Jessica anymore. This is about Rebecca from Texas and Sophie and me. That genie has my cat, and she is going to pay. To get to her, I've decided to go through her kid master. If I can make her fail with Jessica — and the genie council hears about it — hopefully she'll be dethroned. If they had any idea what was really going on here, she'd be kicked out already. I don't know how to tell on her. It isn't a genie's job to know what other genies are up to. And we're never supposed to stay in the same house! I have no idea how any of this happened. But it has — and I'm going to make sure Rebecca from Texas never does anything like this again.

So I told Sophie my plan. "You need to get Jessica in more trouble than she's ever seen in her life."

"Yeah!" Sophie said.

"I want you to do the one thing that will make Jessica miserable. You turn her into the school's biggest loser — and liar." I paused for effect. I thought Sophie would clap or cheer, but she didn't. She just sat there quietly, playing with the silver rings on her fingers.

"What sports season is it? What is she doing the most now?"

"Swimming."

"Okay . . . the night before her next meet, we'll bang on her wall and listen to loud music so she can't sleep a wink. You think she'll win then? She'll never make it to the finish line because she'll never even get into the pool. The next meet . . . do the exact same thing. And do it for the next and the next and the next. Pretty soon, that girl will get kicked off the team. She's a cheerleader, too, right? Well, while she's snoozing through every single swim meet, you can start a rumor that the cheerleading captain has been dropping her teammates on purpose during practices. And guess what you do . . . the night before the next game where she cheers, we keep her awake for hours on end again." I was really on a roll. I stopped to catch my breath. When I looked at Sophie, I could tell she wasn't even paying attention. She looked sad — which was pretty normal lately — and like she was on another frequency altogether.

"So, what do you think, Sophie?"

"Uh, that's great."

"Oh, that sounded enthusiastic. Are you going to do it or what? I'll help you set up your stereo speakers right next to her pillow. Maybe you can somehow play your piccolo in her ear all night, too!"

"Stop!" Whoa, boy. Did I stop. Sophie was raising her voice — probably for the first time in her whole life.

"What?" I asked, still oblivious. I was getting all wound up about our plan to ruin Jessica. Once Rebecca failed miserably on her assignment to make Jess the best at everything, she would be so much easier to destroy and conquer.

"I am not doing any of that. I am not."

"Why not? I'll help you with everything. This will be such a piece of — "

"Genny, what is wrong with you? Are you listening to yourself?"

Well, no, I wasn't.

"You are being as mean and cruel and spiteful as she is. I refuse to do things like that. I want to get her back, but I don't want to stoop to her level. I want to do something that will hurt her, but more importantly, that will make her realize how bad she's being. I have to show her that she's not right, and she's not really a winner. I have to show her that she can't mess with me anymore. I don't want to ruin her life — no matter what she does to me. That's just not how I do things."

Boy, did that shut me up. Sophie was absolutely right, and I was ashamed of myself. I have strict rules about how I can't be mean. And just about three seconds ago, I was very determined to break them. When I get all caught up — and when I'm steamin' mad because someone took my cat — I don't always think clearly. I sure am glad that Sophie was thinking for both of us.

"Genny, if you don't agree, I'm not even sure we're friends."

"Oh my goodness! Don't say that!" I yelled. "I am so sorry. You are absolutely right. I will think of something else immediately. I just haven't gotten much sleep, my cat ran away, and my big toe feels like it needs to be removed. I am so sorry. Please forgive me. I am not thinking clearly."

"Well, of course I forgive you. I am just glad to hear you say that."

"I am just glad you stopped me before I really got on an evil tirade. I never want to end up like that hole-in-her-heart genie Rebecca from Texas!"

"Who?"

"Oh, never mind," I said. I still wasn't sure if I should tell her about Rebecca. Sophie doesn't take well to intimidation. And if I told her what we were up against, she would definitely be intimidated.

We made up. I had to braid her curly hair and paint her nails. But I didn't mind, because I owed it to her. I could tell she was really disappointed in me earlier, and I didn't want her to stay that way. I don't think she did. She played the piccolo for me later before we went to bed. She told me she wished she was back in the eighth-grade band.

I was so tired, all I wanted to do was fall into a deep, snoring, squeaking sleep. I couldn't, no matter how many sheep I counted. I had to think of something to do to that evil Texan wench. Then it dawned on me — while being so mad at her, I had forgotten about the whole reason why I was there. Sophie was still miserable. I had to get her back in that band class and back in her parents' good graces. That was more important than seeking revenge on a brand-new, albeit evil, genie. When I thought about it, that should be easy. She has only been doing assignments for less than a year. I've been at 'em for a little more than a thousand. I don't think there's anything she can dish out that I can't take.

But I can't stand not knowing if she's got my cat, or if she's just teasing me. I hope she's just teasing me. I can't imagine what she'd do to poor fat Catfish. What if she already turned him into a pile of violin strings? I was weak in the knees just thinking about it. I hoped he was okay.

Oh my goodness!

Chapter 25
"What Was It That I Wished For?"
by Jessica

I didn't know that genies had mobile phones until I overheard mine talking to someone on one.

"Yeah, I will be the only genie on earth worth remembering. It will be soon. I just have to get rid of Genny the Genie." There was a pause. "Yeah, I mean that dumb little chick from ancient France who's been riding on her reputation for the last three hundred years. I plan to totally destroy her." Another pause. "It should be easy; she lives in the same house with two gir — "

Just then Rebecca saw me walk in and threw her phone into her bottle. Shoot! I should've stayed outside to listen longer. Now I'm itching to know if she was talking about me and my sister.

"Hiya, gal! What is goin' on with you?"

"I am just coming into my room." I'm sure she could tell I was irritated.

"Good thing you did! I was just thinkin' about you."

"Yeah, sounds like it."

"Don't you worry your pretty little head about my personal business. It's got nothing to do with you."

I guess she's right, I didn't need to know about everything. I decided to believe her. It was easier to love Rebecca than get into a brawl with her, because she gave me every-thing I could ever want. And things were going so well! I was on top of my game at school and at home. I just didn't like hurting Sophie over and over again. Sure, she was more than annoying, but she didn't deserve to be miser-able. But everything we kept doing effectively made Sophie out to be a bad girl. I know her much better than Rebecca does, and I know she is probably so upset that she'd rather eat rusty nails than go through anything else. I'm start-ing to wonder what I wished for. Originally, I just wanted to be the best at my sports at school and make our parents adore me. Look-ing at everything now, I don't feel so great about that. Is that what I should be wishing for?

"Rebecca, I know you took my cat, Furball, into your bottle. But do you think I can have him back?"

"In a bit. I'm not done with him yet."

"Done with him? Listen, I need that cat back."

"Sorry, you'll get him back soon. Don't worry, he's doing fine. He's just lounging around and living the good life inside my bottle, named Earthquake."

I was thisclose to demanding that she give my cat back. But have you seen how psychotic Rebecca from Texas gets when she's mad? Well, just the other day, she left her lipstick on the windowsill, where, duh, the sun melted it. "That was ma fay-vorite lipstick from my fay-vorite store. My momma bought that shade for me!!! Dagnabbit! Doggonnit!! I *neeeed* that stuff."

Boy, she threw one heck of a fit. I just sat there on my bed hoping it would blow over soon.

How many days does she have left with me?

Chapter 26
"Puh-leeze!"
by Genny the Genie

I got the meanest genie-mail today:

Roses are red
Violets are blue
Your cat is dead meat
You are, too
—RfT

If she knows what's good for her, she'd better not do anything cruel and unusual to Catfish. I felt so helpless — and so responsible. I should have figured this all out earlier. I knew this chick was after me. I just didn't dream she'd purposely seek out the same house that I'm in, and prey on another human girl just to get back at me. This was getting sicker by the second.

I know I've told you that I can't cry, but I did it again. A good boo-hoo used to always make me feel better. But I managed to stay strong. It wouldn't matter in a few days — I could take care of her.

She called me dead meat? I don't think so!

I read over my list again. I had made a copy of the Twelve Ways to Trick Your Biggest Enemy and I carried it around in my back pocket. I read it over and over again for inspiration. My own plan was almost complete.

Just wait until I chip my perfectly painted fingernails wringing her proverbial neck. Or her bottle . . . She has no idea who she is messing with. She's going to be wishing she never became a genie in the first place. She's going to be begging me for dear life, if all goes according to my brilliant plan. I know my way around the rules and around the entire genie universe so well, she really doesn't stand a chance. I don't know why I was ever scared. After all, I am not the most famous genie who ever genie'd for nothing!

But what if she knows some newfangled fancy tricks I've never seen before? I hope there haven't been any advances in magic or mind control since I last visited the genie council headquarters. What if she has her own ultra-modern genie guidebook?

That doesn't mean I'm going to worry my ponytail off. I have to keep telling myself that: *Genny, you're not going to worry your ponytail off!* After all, I may be committed to playing fair, but that doesn't mean I play nice.

Catfish, wherever you are, don't you purry. I will be there soon.

First, though, I have something superimportant to do. So I called up my accomplice: a cute little curly-headed dude named Andrew.

"Andrew, my name is Genny and I'm Sophie's friend," I said.

"Yeah?"

"I need you to do something for her. But you can't tell her I told you to do it. With your help, I can get her back in the band."

"Who are you?" he asked.

"I'm her cousin in Indiana," I lied. "But she told me what's been going on — and I thought of a way to really get everything back on track for her. Will you help me out?"

"Sure."

Chapter 27
"Oh My Goodness! Oh My Goodness!"
by Sophie

"Genny, pinch me!" I demanded. "Yee-ouch! Did you have to do it that hard?"

Neither bruises nor bumps nor bloody knees could spoil my mood today. I was up in the clouds and away with the fairies.

See, when I arrived at school today, Mr. Schultz called me into his office. I was running into the bathroom, nearly tripping over my two left feet, when he ordered me to come in. I had to ask him if I could go to the rest room first. I definitely needed to calm down before I went face-to-face with the man who hates me. I was so scared that I was in trouble for something else. For what, I didn't know. But it's not like I expected to become a clarinet thief, either. So I stood in the bathroom and splashed water on my face. I said the alphabet in pig Latin three times — Genny taught me that trick. I felt a little better, and I made my way toward Mr. Schultz's office.

"Sit down, Sophie," he said superternly. "I want you to see something." I thought maybe he'd pull out a smashed-up instrument and tell me I was in trouble for crushing it with a car. I don't drive, though, so maybe it would be something else. Instead of dead clarinets, he pulled out a few sheets of paper. "Read this for me. Go ahead and read it out loud."

Read! What could I have possibly done-that-I-didn't-do this time? I read aloud like he asked me to. " 'Dear Mr. Schultz. We think Sophie O'Bannon is a really good piccolo player. We would love for her to be back in the eighth-grade band class. We don't want to play without her Friday at the winter concert. She adds a lot of talent to our band.

" 'Also, you may not know her as well as we do, but we are sure that she didn't steal your clarinet. In fact, someone on this list — who begged to remain anonymous — saw a girl who wasn't Sophie carrying your special clarinet out of the classroom the day before Sophie got caught. We just hope you'll give her another chance.

" 'She is a really good piccolo player.

" 'Our petition below means that we want her back very badly. We don't think she should be punished anymore.

" 'Sincerely,

" 'Andrew Green, Carolyn Susan, Ronnie Mack, Chandra Michael, Whitney Diaz, Kelly Elizabeth, Joy Gaines, Steve Koss, Kris Lewis, Christie Older, Lia Montrel, Jodi Angeles . . .' " The list went on and on. I just kept reading names.

Then I cried. I had no idea this many people even knew who I was.

"Sophie," Mr. Schultz said, "I think you deserve to be back in the band."

"You do?"

"Yes, and I've decided to give you the benefit of the doubt. I was so shocked and surprised that the clarinet was in your locker. I know there are a lot of kids who might be jealous of you. So I'm going to take the other kids' word for it. I don't believe that you took my prized clarinet."

"Mr. Schultz, I promise that I didn't. I don't even have a clue who did."

"Does anyone have your locker combination?"

"Well," I paused. "No." I still couldn't bring myself to tell anyone that the only person who can get in my locker is Jessica.

"Okay," he went on. "I am calling your parents tonight. You better start practicing for Friday's concert. Actually, I know you've been keeping up on our assignments — I hear you during lunch and after school. I'm still very proud of you, Sophie. I am even giving you a solo on Friday."

"Are you really? Thank you so much!"

I am sure I bounced around — that's what thirteen-year-olds like me do when we're happy. As I made my exit, I remembered one more thing. "Mr. Schultz?"

"Yes?"

"Who did all of this for me?"

"I assume your friend Andrew. He's the one who brought the petition to me."

I did something I hadn't done before; I called him up. He seemed happy to hear from me. "Andrew?"

"Sophie! Hey!" he answered.

"I owe you my piccolo."

"Really, you don't."

"I do! Thank you!"

"Everyone wanted you back, Sophie. Not just me."

"Really?" I couldn't fathom that lots of kids actually knew me. I felt really cool.

"Really, Sophie. It's true."

"I need to say thank you."

"No you don't. You're my best friend and I'd do anything for you."

"I would for you, too," I said.

I spent the night playing and playing and playing the piccolo. I didn't stop until my fingertips were ready to bleed. Genny danced around so happily.

Chapter 28
"This Is Too Much!"
by Jessica

I don't want to be this jealous, but I can't help it. I am! Our parents are fawning all over my silly sister. They are apologizing for being so mean to her. They keep telling her how great and talented and sweet she is. Barf, puke, vomit. What is so big about that dumb piccolo? If she doesn't stop playing it soon, I am going to lose my mind. So is Rebecca. We've been trying to mosh to Metallica; we thought that would make us feel better. But that doggone piccolo — playing the graduation march — just keeps ruining the mood.

"I am so over that annoying girl," Rebecca told me as she placed her twenty-gallon cowgirl hat on my head. She was getting out her honky-tonk CDs next, swearing that they would put us in a better state of mind.

"Me, too. I win how many meets? I do how

many great things? And what do I get to show for it? Nothing!"

"Well, we can take care of that."

She poofed into her bottle, and I heard a screeching meow that turned my stomach. Before I had a chance to rub three times to get her out, she poofed back into my room on her own.

"What was going on in there?"

"Oh, nothing. Listen, don't interrupt me for a second. I have a grand plan," she said, rubbing her fingers together. "As soon as your sister goes to sleep, I'm going in her room and stealing her piccolo."

"Didn't we already steal something once?"

"Don't worry — I'm taking it back to her. It's just that I'm rubbing poison ivy all over it first. Then we'll see how well she plays in two days. That will teach her to mess with us!"

I was more jealous than I'd ever felt in my life, so the plan sounded good at the time. In my rage, I didn't care how we took care of her. I just wanted her to get out of my spotlight. Boy, was I eaten up with the green-eyed monster, as my mother calls it. I got out my pogo stick to let off steam. I hopped around in my room until I broke a really big sweat. Then I started to feel better.

"I want my cat back. I am demanding that you give me Furball."

"No. I love Furball now, and he's mine." She told me a sob story about how her childhood kitty recently had died, and she cried and cried. Rebecca went on about how lonely it is in that bottle, and how she needed a companion of her own. Well, how did she think I felt? Furball was my closest friend, too! She bawled some more and begged. I started to feel bad — but I vowed to try to get that special guy back eventually.

I left my room for dinner, but I couldn't eat. My mom made Sophie's favorite Italian dish — homemade pepperoni pizza. I tried to smile and be a good sport, but I couldn't swallow another bite. I excused myself from the table early. I heard some talking — it must've been Rebecca — so this time I stood outside my door to listen. Maybe I shouldn't have.

"I am so over these twin girls. I've never heard problems so dumb," she said into her mobile phone. "Yes, I am almost done with them. They are just getting me closer and closer to my goal. I am wiping out that Genny the Genie — she's the other sister's genie . . . Oh yeah . . . Uh-huh . . ."

The skin that goes around the outside of my ears started to tingle. Did that mean that Rebecca never really liked me much all along?

Did that mean she was using me? I don't think I like being a pawn — no matter how many cool and expensive gifts I get.

Her conversation went on. "I'm getting to that genie through her cat . . . yeah, I've got him locked up in my bottle. She won't even recognize him; he's so skinny. . . . Ha! Ha! Ha! When? Oh, well, I'm sure the poof-off will be today."

Could this day possibly get any worse?

I think I hate my genie.

Chapter 29
"I'll Show Her"
by Genny the Genie

Sophie is such a sweetie! I am sad that I have to leave her soon. Only two days before my time is *really* up. And so much left to do! I hope she finds her piccolo; we searched all over for it this morning. She thinks she just misplaced it. Well, I have to help her find it in the next two days. She has a concert, and I have to pack up. Thank my Throttle that I've just about finished everything there is to do here. I only have two more items of unfinished business. One: I have to rescue my cat. Two: I will stop Rebecca. I have just enough time.

Ahhh, this is very important and exciting business, too. A mean genie like Rebecca can't hide her evil self for long. I know that the genie council will get her soon enough. The last time we had a bad genie, she was barely out of genie school before she got put in the poofer. This Rebecca is smarter than she was. She hides her dark side from everyone but her targets. That will get you quite far if you keep stamping out your enemies. She can't stamp out me, though. Many have tried. But does it look like they succeeded?

Besides, she is hurting the Sophies and Jessicas of the world while she goes after what she wants. That is why I can't wait for the genie council to take care of her. I hope I don't get in too much trouble for getting involved, but I feel like I have to. If she were after only supernatural beings like me, I'd wait and let the council punish her. But she's made the big mistake of involving kids. Not to mention that she stole my cat. *No one* steals my cat.

I've pored over the books. I've consulted the cosmos. I asked my dead papa's spirit for wisdom and advice to guide me. To be completely honest, though, I came up with the scheme on my own.

First, I sent her a genie-mail after the girls went to school.

To RfT,
Meet me outside in ten minutes . . . if you're brave enough. Bring your bottle. If you show up

without it, the poof-off is off. Don't worry, I will bring mine as well.

I'm wishing you luck now because you're going to need it.

Adieu,

Genny the Genie

I told Throttle that he was on his own. I was going to be too busy knocking her into submission to protect him. As you know, if she gets my bottle, this whole thing is over. If I get her bottle, this whole thing is over. But I'm not worried about that. She may not realize that while Throttle is old, he is quick and smart. No one will ever be able to capture him. Hopefully, though, I can get my hands on hers.

We met underneath a big old oak tree.

"You're older than the dirt in the ground," she said to me when we met face-to-face for the second time. I was struck by her eyes. Those mean, dark things will haunt me for the rest of my eternal life.

"You have chosen to mess with someone who has seen every trick in the book. I assure you that you have gone down the wrong road."

"You don't scare me, Genny."

We hovered around each other like boxers in a ring. She looked ready to strike. I wasn't ready to go genie-on-genie yet, so I dead-eyed her while I kept my distance. I left Throttle on the ground beside me. She looked at him, smiling a sinister, evil grin. I wasn't worried about him. Obviously, though, she was worried about her bottle. She had him in a pouch that was draped across her chest. The screeching, scratching, and meowing was the sweetest sound I'd heard in weeks. Well, besides Sophie's piccolo playing, that is.

"Ahhh, that's what I want to hear," I said. "Catfish, Genny is right here." He made those long, deep, desperate meows that cats do when they're at death's door. He did it over and over — it didn't stop. Rebecca was going nuts. "Shut up! Shut up! I'll reach in there and rip your whiskers out if I have to hear another sound!"

"Meeeerrrrrrrrr-OWWWW! Meeeerrrrrrrr-OWWWW! MeeerrrrrrrOWWWWW! Meeer-rrrrrrrOWWWWWW! Meeerrrrrrrrrr-OWWWWWW!"

I smiled. Catfish is good at pushing buttons.

"Nee-how, blee-how, see-how," I began to chant repetitively as I hovered and halfway closed my eyes.

"Your stupid spells don't scare me. I think they're pathetic. I know you're just playing a game."

She shouldn't be so sure. Some of my spells actually work.

She reached for my ponytail and pulled it. I just let her. She swung at my eyes. Again, I just let her. She got in a few good punches, but I didn't care. Making her think she was winning was part of the plan. I acted like I was beaten up and tired. That's when she — predictably — reached for Throttle. As soon as her hand got close, he scooted just out of reach, giggling. I hate when he does that to me — so I laughed when he pulled such a simple trick on her.

At this point, she was bent over with her back slightly to me. I gave her a swift little kick in the heinie. "That's for Sophie."

She toppled over, but came back to life. She wiggled her fingers at me as if she could actually do magic. "Take that!" I heard something that sounded like a blown TV. Then I felt it.

Oh my goodness.

Whatever came out of her fingers knocked me to the ground. She *did* have magical powers. Maybe that's why she got to be the Year 2000 genie. I got special treatment because I was so smart and sweet. She got it because she's got this gift. It was all starting to make sense. I sure hoped my smarts would kick in soon. The old stealing-her-bottle strategy wasn't going to work.

After being zapped so rudely, my head really hurt. I noticed that Throttle had disappeared.

That was not a good sign. He never gets scared. At least he got out of the way fast so she couldn't strike him next. That would definitely be the end of me.

"Nee-how. Blee-how. Bee-how." Okay, so I wasn't casting a spell. I do admit that I was up to something. She thought I was reaching up to pull her hair, which I did. But only because I needed a strand. Meanwhile, I grabbed for her bottle; it was still very firmly strapped to her chest. I could tell whatever magic she had just done to me wore her out. She was definitely a little weaker than before.

I let her punch me four more times, then I positioned myself by a tree.

"You are such a loser. I can't believe they ever made you a genie," I taunted. Since she's a young genie hothead, I could tell she was getting really poofed at me. That was good, so I kept going. "I heard you lied your way into the geniehood. I even heard that you're already about to get kicked out." All lies, of course, but she was falling for them. She raised her hands and got ready to shock me again. "You look terrible, girlfriend. I've never seen such bad clothes and tacky triple-processed hair in my whole entire life. And I've had a long — "

Blam! She tried to shock me again, but she hit the tree I hid behind. The bark was smoking.

Boy, I'm glad I missed that. Just as I hoped, she was weakened.

"Nee-how? Blee-how? Bee-how?" With those words, Throttle appeared on a branch. I put Rebecca's hair into it. She reached for him, and he disappeared. Like she really had a chance to grab him.

We hovered and duked it out again for a while. I yelled, "Throttle, come back." He showed up on the ground, where I hovered, protecting him. He had a piece of Rebecca's hair, which meant he had the power to do one trick. "Do it," I said.

Her pouch disappeared, and her bottle fell to the ground. She was really freaked.

"You little sneak. You don't know what you're doing. You'll be sorry," she ranted and raved as her bottle tumbled to the ground next to mine. I had them both directly underneath me. She'd have to magic me again with her hands to get her bottle back. I knew she was going to do it again any second, so I worked fast.

I reached into my jeans pocket, and threw a couple of Q-Tips into her shiny new bottle. That's all my kitty needed. . . .

"MEOW!" Catfish was able to jump out. See, Q-Tips are the things that make my genie cat able to do whatever he wants. They give him superpowers that I don't have. Why he was granted Q-Tip magic, I don't know. I'm just glad his Q-Tips enabled him to escape. He was rail-skinny. I told him, "Jump into Throttle and get some pizza." He did it. "Whew!" I knew at least he was safe.

BAM!

She got me again, and I fell to the ground. Before Throttle had a chance to swallow her bottle, she grabbed it back. Darn! That wasn't the plan!

She chased me around the yard and zapped me some more. I was just about to retreat and regroup with Throttle. I had to save up some energy and plan for Attack Number Two. Then I heard some girls' voices nearby.

"Take that!" one of them said. A slingshot with a rubber ball knocked Rebecca's bottle out of her hand. A girl ran over and got it. Never did I think I'd be glad to see Jessica. She held the bottle while Rebecca stared at her.

"Don't you do it, Jess," Rebecca said. "Don't you rub that bottle three times. If I have to go inside my bottle right now, you'll ruin everything."

"I won't if you give me back my cat this second," she said.

"I don't have the cat. That wench over there took him."

With that, Jess rubbed Rebecca's bottle three

times. *Poof!* She was gone. I jumped up and down. I clapped because I wouldn't have to get zapped. I expected Jessica to carry the bottle inside the house and do who-knows-what with it. But then she walked straight up to me. I could see Sophie standing in the doorway.

"Here," she said as she handed Rebecca in a Bottle to me.

"Me? How can you see me?" I asked her.

"Sophie let me see you. And I let Sophie see Rebecca. We wanted to get rid of her, too."

"Thank you."

Rebecca started screaming from inside her bottle. "Jessica, you rub me three times right now. I'm commanding you. If you don't, I'll take all of the stuff I gave you to the dump. I'll burn you alive! I swear."

"Shut up, Rebecca," I said. "You're not Jessica's anymore. You're mine." I put her bottle — she was still screaming inside it — into Throttle. He and Catfish and I could now keep her contained for all eternity. I just hoped we wouldn't have to listen to her scream for the rest of our lives. We'd better invest in some earplugs.

I looked inside the house, where I saw Sophie and Jessica hugging. It looked like they were making up. Maybe Rebecca came here for a reason. I know I did. Anyway, Jessica was washing Sophie's piccolo for her with soap. Then she dried it really well. Then she sat down and polished it. How sweet is that?

They came back outside to talk to me. I was laid out flat underneath that tree. I could barely get up, I was that exhausted. Throttle was resting on the other side of the yard — I had to put him far away from me because I couldn't stand Rebecca's yelling.

"Genny," Sophie began to say, "can you come to my concert tomorrow?"

"Oh no! I have to leave tomorrow. My twenty-eight days are up!"

"Can't you break the rules like you did before?" Sophie asked.

"This time, honey, I can't. Jessica, you'll go in my place, right?"

"I would love to," she said as she grabbed Sophie's hand. "I wouldn't miss it."

Chapter 30
"I Will Try Harder"
by Jessica

I have been mean to my sister.

If there is one thing I've learned from Rebecca from Texas, it is not to be mean to other people. I am glad I met her because if I hadn't, maybe I would have turned out as mean and hateful as she is. That would be scary. I am sure that I was turning into Rebecca.

Being the best isn't always the best — that's what I've decided.

I have apologized to my sister Sophie (the future music composer) for everything I've done to her in the past year. I told her that I will still be jealous of her and her piccolo — I just can't help it. But I will try to be kind about it. I promised her that I will try. I will, too. I am determined to do that, and you know how I get when I set my mind on something. I can't believe she already said she'd forgive me. Wait a minute — sure I can believe it. After all, she's

Sophie! She's the girl who still believes in the Good Ship Lollipop.

She is the best friend anyone could ever have. I am lucky that she is not only my friend, but also my sister.

About the Author

Kristen Kemp is the author of several books about Genny the Genie, as well as other Scholastic titles, such as the 2 Grrrls guides. She stays busy writing for women's and teen magazines and is currently a contributing editor at *YM*. She lives in Saratoga Springs, NY, with her husband, Steve, their dog, Clipper, and two cats. In her spare time, she loves to visit her hometown in Indiana.